W9-ASQ-292

'JAN 3 1 2011'

SHORT TALES
Furlock & Muttson Mysteries

THE Case OF
THE MiSSiNG GOLDFiSH

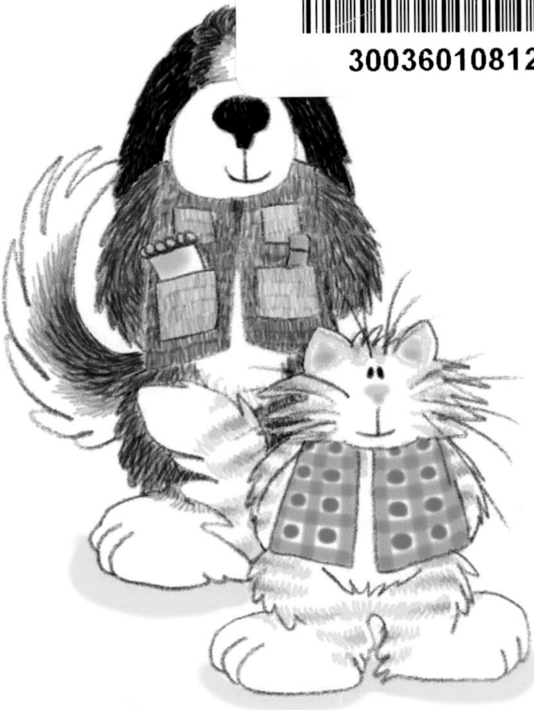

by Robin Koontz

visit us at www.abdopublishing.com

Published by Magic Wagon, a division of the ABDO Group, 8000 West 78th Street, Edina, Minnesota, 55439. Copyright © 2010 by Abdo Consulting Group, Inc. International copyrights reserved in all countries.

Short Tales ™ is a trademark and logo of Magic Wagon.

Printed in the United States of America, North Mankato, Minnesota.
092009
012010

Written and illustrated by Robin Koontz
Edited by Stephanie Hedlund and Rochelle Baltzer
Interior Layout by Kristen Fitzner Denton
Book Design and Packaging by Shannon Eric Denton

Library of Congress Cataloging-in-Publication Data

Koontz, Robin Michal.
   The case of the missing goldfish / written and illustrated by Robin Koontz.
      p. cm. -- (Short tales. Furlock & Muttson mysteries)
   ISBN 978-1-60270-561-6
   [1. Goldfish--Fiction. 2. Mystery and detective stories.] I. Title.
   PZ7.K83574Casm 2010
   [E]--dc22
                                        2008032533

"Good morning, Furlock," said Muttson.
"How are you?"
"I am tired," Furlock said. "I stayed up late
reading my detective comics."
"Take a nap," said Muttson. "I will answer the
telephone if it rings."

Soon, the telephone rang.
"Furlock and Muttson Detective Agency,"
Muttson said.
"Uh-huh, I see. We are on our way,
Mrs. Bumblebear!" Muttson said.

"What has happened?" Furlock asked.
"Goldie the goldfish is missing!" Muttson said.
"Goldfish?" Furlock licked her lips.
"Stop that!" cried Muttson. "It is our job to find Goldie, not eat her!"

Furlock jumped to her feet.
"Fire up the Furlock-Mobile!" she said.
They sped to the house of Mrs. Bumblebear.

Mrs. Bumblebear met them at her door.
"Thank goodness you are here!" she said.
"Don't worry, we will find your goldfish,"
said Furlock.

"What does she look like?" asked Furlock.
"She is a gold fish," said Mrs. Bumblebear.
"Goldfish is gold," Muttson said quietly.
He wrote on his notepad.

"Where did you see her last?" Furlock asked.
"She was in her fishbowl," Mrs. Bumblebear said.
She led them to the fishbowl on a small table.
"Someone spilled water on the table," said Furlock.
"Water on the table," Muttson said, taking notes.

Furlock noticed a cup of water on a chair
next to the table.
"Someone did not finish this water," she said.
"What does that mean?" cried Mrs. Bumblebear.

"I am not sure," said Furlock. "We must look for more clues."
Furlock peeked into a doorway next to the chair.

"Is this the kitchen?" she asked.
"Yes," said Mrs. Bumblebear.
Furlock saw a bag of bread, a bag of cookies,
and a box of plastic bags.

"Someone made a sandwich," she said.
Muttson nodded.

Furlock saw another doorway next to the first.
"Is that the bathroom?" she asked.
"Yes," said Mrs. Bumblebear.

Furlock looked
at the fishbowl
on the table.

She looked
at the cup
on the chair.

"Aha!"
she said.

"Muttson, poke in the toilet for a goldfish!"
"No way!" cried Muttson. "If Goldie were in the
toilet, we would see her."

"You are right," said Furlock.
"Now the case is solved."
"Oh," said Muttson. "Yes, I see."

"Goldie jumped from her fishbowl to the cup?" asked Mrs. Bumblebear.

"That is correct," said Furlock.

"And then she jumped from the cup to the toilet?"

"Yes," said Furlock, "and I am afraid that
someone flushed."
"Oh dear! Oh dear!" Mrs. Bumblebear cried.
"Kippy will be heartbroken!"

"Who is Kippy?" asked Muttson.
"Kippy is my son," said Mrs. Bumblebear.

"He was so happy this morning,"
Mrs. Bumblebear said. "Today
was show-and-tell!"

Muttson stared at his notepad.
"Furlock! I think we have it all wrong!" he said.

"What did I miss?" asked Furlock.
"You did not miss a thing," Muttson said.
"Do you remember the plastic bags
in the kitchen?"

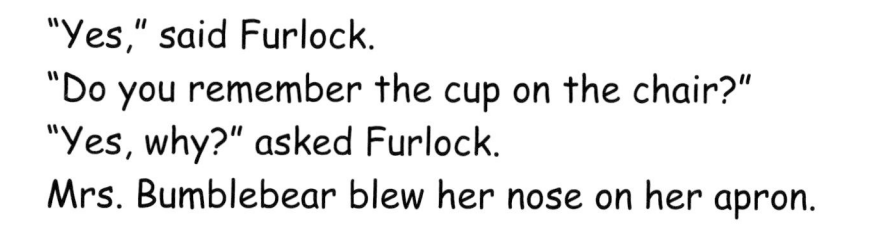

"Yes," said Furlock.

"Do you remember the cup on the chair?"

"Yes, why?" asked Furlock.

Mrs. Bumblebear blew her nose on her apron.

"I think Kippy made more than a sandwich,"
said Muttson. "I think he took Goldie for
show-and-tell!"
"How?" Furlock asked.

"He scooped her from the fishbowl with the cup," said Muttson. "Then he poured her in a plastic bag."
"That must be it!" said Mrs. Bumblebear.
She went to call the school.

"I hope I am right," said Muttson. "It would be better than Goldie getting flushed."
"You mean, you hope we are right," said Furlock.

Mrs. Bumblebear came running back.
"You were right!" she said. "Kippy took Goldie to
school for show-and-tell! Thank you so much!"
"We are happy to help," said Furlock.

"Would you like some breakfast?"
asked Mrs. Bumblebear.
"That sounds lovely," said Furlock.
"Can you make tuna fish pancakes?"

"Yuck!" cried Muttson. "Furlock, we need to go back to the office. We may have another case."

"Have the bag of honey cookies,"
said Mrs. Bumblebear.
"Thank you very much!" said Furlock.
She popped a cookie in her mouth.
"Muththon, on thoo thuh neth caseth!"
"I am right behind you," said Muttson.

They jumped into the Furlock-Mobile
and sped away.